The Year Without a Santa Claus

by Phyllis McGinley ★ illustrated by John Manders

SCHOLASTIC INC.
New York Toronto London Auckland
Sydney Mexico City New Delhi Hong Kong

D0478333

In memory of Phyllis McGinley

For Angelina, who is surely on Santa's "Good" list
—J.M.

No part of this publication may be reproduced, stored in a retrieval system, or transmitted in any form or by any means, electronic, mechanical, photocopying, recording, or otherwise, without written permission of the publisher. For information regarding permission, write to Marshall Cavendish Corporation, 99 White Plains Road, Tarrytown, NY 10591.

ISBN 978-0-545-38313-4

Text copyright © 1956, 1957 by Phyllis McGinley, renewed 1984 by Patricia Hayden Blake. Reprinted in cooperation with Patricia Hayden and Curtis Brown, Ltd. Illustrations copyright © 2010 by John Manders. All rights reserved. Published by Scholastic Inc., 557 Broadway, New York, NY 10012, by arrangement with Marshall Cavendish Corporation. SCHOLASTIC and associated logos are trademarks and/or registered trademarks of Scholastic Inc.

12 11 10 9 8 7 6 5 4 3 2 1   11 12 13 14 15 16/0

Printed in the U.S.A.   08

This edition first printing, September 2011

Although the text is faithful to the author's original poem, the spelling and punctuation have been altered in a few spots for readability.

The illustrations were rendered in Winsor & Newton's gouache with line work in Prismacolor pencil, on Arches 300 lb. hot press watercolor paper.
Book design by Anahid Hamparian
Editor: Marilyn Brigham

Lexile is a registered trademark of MetaMetrics, Inc.

Have you been told?

Did you ever hear
of the
curious
furious
fidgety year
when Santa Claus
unhitched his sleigh
and vowed he was taking a holiday?

How did it happen?
This way:
It was long ago
before you were living—
not yet Christmas but past Thanksgiving,
though I can't give you the very date.

Santa got up that morning,
late;
pulled on one boot,
then its twin,
ruffled the whiskers on his chin
and sat back down on the side of the bed.
"Great North Star, but I'm tired!"
he said.
"Painting wagons
red and bright,
sharpening ice skates half the night,
wrapping presents in ribbons and gauze,
has worn me weary,"
said Santa Claus.

"Crick in my back,
cold in my nose,
aches in my fingers and all ten toes,
and a sort of a kind of a kink
inside,
whenever I think
of that Christmas Ride."

Into his workroom limped the Saint.
He sniffed the varnish,
he smelled the paint.
And a reeling
feeling
came over him stealing
to see things crammed from floor to ceiling:

Rocking horses with shaggy manes,
balls,
dolls,
electric trains,
gloves, mitts,
doctor's kits,
rubber boots,
cowboy suits,
kites for flying in parks,
bicycles,
Noah's Arks.
And he started to shake and he started to shiver
at thought of the load he must soon deliver.

And he sighed, "Oh, dear!"
as he buttoned his vest.
"I wish *one* year
I could take a rest."

When the words were out
he stood stock-still.
And then he whispered,
"I think . . . I . . . will!
I will," he cried with his eyes ablaze.
"Everyone else gets holidays:
Sailors and
tailors and
cooks do,
policemen
and writers of books do;
tamers of lions and leopards,
preachers and
teachers and
shepherds;
watchmen,
Scotchmen,
Spaniards,
Turks;

butchers and bakers and grocery clerks—
they take time off as Christmas nears.
All except me.
So it appears
that, saint or not,
it's time I got
my first vacation in a thousand years."

Out in the stable, nuzzling hay,
the reindeer dreamed of Christmas Day.

But Santa phoned to the reindeer groom,
"Hang up the harness
in the big store room."

He called to his Elves,
he told each Gnome,
"Cover up the shelves!
We're staying home."

"What! Cover the shelves?"
cried Gnomes and Elves.
"Cover the dolls and electric trains
and the rocking horses with shaggy manes
and the rubber boots
for splashing in parks
and the cowboy suits
and the Noah's Arks?
Alas! Alack!"
For they couldn't believe
he wouldn't go riding
on Christmas Eve.

"Put 'em away," roared Santa, vexed.
"This year's presents will do for next.
Warn the people,
tell the papers,
I'm much too tired for Christmas capers.
Crick in my back,
a cold that lingers,
aches in my toes and all ten fingers,
bit of lumbago,
touch of gout,
climbing down chimneys is simply out.
I may be the saint of the children's nation
but this is the year
of my first vacation."

Well, you can imagine,

more or less

what happened when *that* news reached the Press.

Headlines screamed,

wires went humming,

SANTA SAYS "TOO TIRED"

NOT COMING

And as the word

flashed far and wide

you should have *heard*

how the children cried!

So violently they sobbed their griefs

the shops ran out of handkerchiefs.

Their tears filled up the kitchen sinks

and cellars and empty skating rinks.

They wept in school;

at play they wept.

They dampened their pillows while they slept.

Before those darlings' eyes got drier,

all the rivers rose three feet higher.

And I don't know what would have happened,

quite,

except for Ignatius Thistlewhite.

Ignatius Thistlewhite was a boy
in Texas (or was it Illinois?)
six years old,
but brave for his years,
he sobbed no sobs
and he wept no tears
but stood up tall in his class
to say,
"Santa *deserves* a holiday!"

"No, no, no!"
came the children's plaint.
"What is Christmas without our saint?"

"Shucks, now, fellows!
Gosh, Good Gracious!
Christmas is *Christmas*,"
cried Ignatius.
"And everyone tells me, whom I've met,
it's a day to give,
as well as to get.
Since all these years
in the children's cause,
Santa's been giving without one pause,
let's pull together
in the Christmas weather
and give this year
to Santa Claus!"

"Hooray," his classmates said.
"He's right!
Three cheers for Ignatius Thistlewhite!"

Fast as a hurricane, children hurled
that happy message around the world,
over each continent,
isle, and isthmus:
"Let's give Santa a Merry Christmas."

With snow the Earth was already whit'ning.
But they rolled up their sleeves
and worked like lightning.
They opened their piggy banks,
racked their brains.
They chartered buses and special trains
and ships and sledges
and hydroplanes,

to reach the Pole
by the 24th
was all their goal.

East, south, west, north,
came gifts and gifts and gifts to spare
from clever children everywhere:

Slippers
with zippers
to zip on;
soap for his bath
or to slip on;
geraniums pink in a pot;
one guppy;
a puppy
named Spot;
balsam pillows,
strawberry jam,
dressing gowns with his monogram;
ten harmonicas for him to play on,
hand-painted pictures
done in crayon,
mufflers, pipes,
an easy chair,
and lots of winter underwear.
In New York State
a boy called Pudge
cooked him a plate
of homemade fudge.

And little Girl Guides of Britain
each made him a scarlet mitten,
while a boy in Siam
sent a Siamese kitten.

They sent him lemon drops
by the carton;
ashtrays modeled in kindergarten;
jackknives, pen-wipers,
cakes and crullers,
and magic pencils that wrote three colors.

Tots who hadn't a penny to spend,
wrote him letters signed:
"A FRIEND."

And they had more fun, that strange December
(they said) than any they could remember.

Up at the Pole, in the fragrant hay,
the idle reindeer dreamed at play.
Comet nickered for oats and corn,
Dancer brandished his velvet horn,
while sadly, sorrily, lounged at home
each idle Elf and Gnome.
Santa sat poking the fire, and blinking,
but nobody knew what he was thinking.

Then suddenly, from the sky
there came the sound of planes.
He heard the hoot and the cry
of ships and special trains.
"Noel!" tootled the sledges,
"Honk!" the buses cried,
and out of his study window
Santa put his head.
He looked to the left.
He stared to the right.
He didn't trust his own eyesight,
so many, so merry,
so more and more
packages were rolling to his front door.
Smack at his doorsill they thundered,

a million!
A thousand!
A hund'erd!

Flat ones and
fat ones and
lean ones;
crimson and silver and green ones,
broad ones

odd ones
plain
romantic ones,
little and big
and great GIGANTIC ones;
parcels from London
Rome
Atlanta
and each addressed alike: "TO SANTA."

Atop them all a banner glinted
where Ignatius Thistlewhite had printed
these words:

"Good luck and holiday mirth
from all the children upon the Earth."

With toots and hoots
and honks lighthearted
the buses turned and the trains departed,
leaving the Saint surrounded by
parcels piled to the Polar sky.

Santa was silent for a minute.
His eye looked bright
but a tear stood in it.
Then he blew his nose like a trumpet blast.
"God bless my soul!"
he said at last.
"By the Big Borealis!
By my maps and charts!
I didn't know children had such kind hearts.
How could a man feel gladder, prouder?"

He turned to his staff
and his voice got louder.
"Gnomes! Elves! Every mother's son!
Don't stand staring,
there's work to be done.
Bring in the barrels,
fetch in the boxes,
carry in those packages
and don't break one!"

Where to put them?
There wasn't space
in parlor or study or *any* place.

They overflowed bureau, couch, and table,
filled the house
the sheds,
the stable;
slid from mantels, jammed the casement,
bulged from attic
and burst from basement.

"There's nothing to do,"
exclaimed the Elves,
"except to empty some workshop shelves."

Off those shelves, then, Santa's forces
whisked the painted rocking horses.
When the presents wouldn't fit,
down came kite and doctor's kit.

Still there wasn't room for all
so away went basketball,
cowboy suit,
rubber boot,
bicycle, and talking doll.

Till by the time that twilight reigned
not a single toy on the shelves remained.
All were sacked and packed away
in the one place left—
the Christmas sleigh.

Then Santa gazed from floor to rafter
and gave his mightiest shout of laughter;
laughed loud ho-ho's,
laughed vast ha-ha's.
"What a joke," he chortled,
"on Santa Claus."

"You might as well phone the reindeer groom
to take down the harness
in the big store room.
Get me my gloves,
the robe for my lap,
and my coat and my warmest stocking cap.
There sits the sleigh
with the toys inside.
So what can I do tonight,
but ride?"

"What about your gout?"
the Gnomes cried out.
"What about your aches and the crick in your spine?"

"Pooh!" laughed Santa,

"My back feels fine!

Never felt younger,

never felt stronger.

Haven't got a symptom any longer.

And before the midnight bells go chiming

I'd like to do some chimney climbing.

So harness the reindeer,

let 'em rip!

It's time to begin my favorite trip."

With flurry and scurry
and chatter and hurry
they brought him his cap and his lap robe furry.
They roused up Cupid,
they rubbed down Vixen.
They polished the bells on Donner and Blixen.
There were cheers from the Gnomes;
from the Elves, applause.
Then off through the night flew Santa Claus.

And I've heard the old people often say
there *never* was such a Christmas Day.
Never such joy after Santa'd swirled
from rooftop to rooftop around the world.
While at the home of a sleepy boy
in Texas (or was it Illinois?)
a special letter was left that night
addressed to
"IGNATIUS THISTLEWHITE."
It was clipped to the handlebars (like a medal)
of the best two-wheeler
a boy could pedal.

"Dear Sir,"
was written in Santa's hand.
"Please thank the children in every land.
Tell them I'll take good care, I hope,
of the guppy
and the puppy
and the slippery soap.
I like my pipes,
I love my chair,
I do appreciate the underwear.
And I pledge this promise on my sled and pack:
year after year
I'll be coming back.

Vacations, I guess, weren't meant for me.
I'll never want another one.

Yours,
S.C."

And that's one reason, you may believe,
why children are merry on Christmas Eve.
You know, yourself,
as you hang your stocking
it doesn't matter if the winds are knocking.
Though the storm falls heavy,
though the great gale roars,
though nobody else would budge outdoors,
snug in your bed while the tempest drums
you can count your blessings
on fingers and thumbs,

for yearly, newly,
faithfully, truly,
somehow
Santa Claus
ALWAYS COMES.